Richard Griffin Starke

The Lord of Lanoraie

A Canadian Legend

Richard Griffin Starke

The Lord of Lanoraie
A Canadian Legend

ISBN/EAN: 9783741186721

Manufactured in Europe, USA, Canada, Australia, Japa

Cover: Foto ©Andreas Hilbeck / pixelio.de

Manufactured and distributed by brebook publishing software
(www.brebook.com)

Richard Griffin Starke

The Lord of Lanoraie

A CANADIAN LEGEND.

... BY ...

RICHARD GRIFFIN STARKE

PRINTED AND PUBLISHED BY
JOHN LOVELL & SON
MONTREAL

PREFACE.

Clinging to the seigniorial mansions of the old Province of Quebec are tale and legend, often of a highly romantic character,—remains of a period in our Colonial history but little known or understood by the general reader, especially from a social point of view. The transition from French to British rule left the old feudal system of land tenure undisturbed, and retained until a much later period many of the quaint usages of the past; and the seigniories were not infrequently acquired by early British colonists by purchase, and occasionally through the marriage tie.

The abandoned, but picturesquely situated Manor-House of Lanoraie, near the village of that name on the North shore of the St. Lawrence, seen many years since by the writer, and which has now entirely disappeared, suggested, with some fragments of legendary lore, the tale embodied in the following pages.

The incidental visit of Prince William Henry, Duke of Clarence, to the St. Lawrence, in command of the warship Pegasus in the summer of 1787, and his sojourn at Sorel, on the opposite shore, and in the vicinity of Lanoraie, afforded further interesting material with which to embellish the story; especially as the Prince had been entertained, if not by the Seigneur of Lanoraie, of which there is nothing now certain, at least by one or more of the neighboring squires. For the purposes of poetry this appears to the writer to be sufficient, his object not being to write history, but as far as may be an interesting fiction.

The author desires further to state that the hero of the tale, the Seigneur of Lanoraie, is not drawn from the life, and has no reference whatever to any real person.

The reader conversant with Canadian history, will also readily understand the writer has used the names Le Moyne d'Iberville, d'Hertel de Rouville, Chartier de Lotbinière, de Ramezay, etc., merely as representative Seigniorial names, and not historically, as to date.

To those of antiquarian tastes it will not be out of place to state that Lanoraie derives its name from Sieur Louis Niort de la Noraye, who, with others, first settled on these lands in 1688, under a patent from Louis XIV. It remained in possession of their heirs till 1724, was acquired by Sieur Jean Baptiste Neveu, and was purchased from his son François Neveu in 1771, by the Honorable James Cuthbert, the then Seigneur of Berthier, who bequeathed it to his third son, the late Honorable Ross Cuthbert, from whom it has descended to his several heirs and still remains in their possession.

As the poem is in the narrative form, and refers to a period which has long passed away, the author has found it more convenient and judged it more effective that the characters themselves should relate the whole story in their proper persons than if it were told in the person of the writer.

If the poem of Lanoraie should induce other writers, more gifted and youthful, to enter this rich field of Canadian romance, one purpose of its publication will at least have been served.

The Author desires warmly to express literary obligations to Mr. and Mrs. William D. Lighthall for enthusiastic interest and friendly criticism in the course of writing and preparing the poem for publication.

THE AUTHOR.

MONTREAL, 1898.

THE LORD OF LANORAIE

INTRODUCTION.

'Twas night, but darkness had not thrown
　Her sombre veil across the sky;
The harvest moon resplendent shone
　High in the azure canopy;

When deep in pensive thought I strayed
　Down by St. Lawrence' placid tide,
Beneath the stately elms that made
　Shadowy aisles on every side.

Scarce noted I the path that drew
　My heedless steps, which way it led;
Far other land my spirit knew,
　And soon the silvery scene had fled.

For now beneath the sunny beam
  Of fair Italia's clime I roved,
Discoursing lore of hill and stream,
  Companioned by the one I loved.

Again we lingered in the vale
  Till came the stars by twilight led,
And poured the ever tuneful tale,
  By clustering vines o'ercanopied.

"Oh love! thou pleasing, anxious thrill,
  Caught from a tone, a look, a sigh,
Or touch, more evanescent still,
  When once thou art, thou canst not die."

I murmured to the midnight air,
  In reverie absorbed I ween,
And now a rustling movement near
  Recalled my thoughts unto the scene.

Some fledgling of these silvan ways
  My steps disturbed, conjecture ran,
I raised my head, my startled gaze
  Fell on the figure of a man.

An agèd, venerable face
  Turned unto me enquiring eyes;
So strangely met in time and place,
  I could but pause in mute surprise.

Close to my steps he sat and leant
Upon a rock of granite grey,
Full in the light, each lineament
Was clear as in the beam of day.

Grey, dusky locks descending dressed
A forehead broad and features high;
A snowy beard flowed down his breast;
Mild were the glances of his eye.

A visage with a look benign
From all the toils of passion free,
And on it dwelt in every line
A graceful pleasing dignity.

His form, once large, was shrunk to half
That it had been in earlier day,
But shapely still, as hat and staff
Upon the rock beside him lay.

Abashed to view that reverend face,—
And truly 'twas a noble sight,—
I paid, at length, with awkward grace,
The salutation of the night.

"A lovely night indeed," he said,
And musing glanced upon the flood,
And on the vault of blue o'erhead,
As if on these he loved to brood.

And still the fascination grew
  The while he spoke and gazed around
Upon a scene so fair to view;
  I stood as on enchanted ground.

"Your pardon, Sir, but may I know
  By what kind chance," continued he,
"This meeting is ? pray you allow
  An old man's curiosity.

"For I have sat full many an hour,
  Between the midnight and the dawn,
Upon this silent moonlit shore,
  Nor oft have met the form of man.

"And now to greet a stranger here
  At this lone hour may well excite
Surprise in one, long worshipper
  And sole companion of the night."

"A wakeful disposition, Sir,
  Disturbed me as at eve I lay,
A traveller at the village there,
  My resting place since yesterday.

"And I, despairing of repose,
  And seeing that the night was clear,
And the moon beautiful, arose
  To view the scene and wander here."

I said, as jealously I thought
   The secret of my heart to hide
And learn the history I sought;
   But soon the pensive man replied.

" And yet, my friend, 'twere strange that you
   Should wander in these paths alone
At midnight hour, if but to view
   The brightness of the harvest moon.

" But trust my motive and confide
   The burthen of your heart to me,
Whose bark has sailed life's troubled tide
   And must ere long at anchor be.

" Consider that some garnered thing
   May be within my humble store
Of wisdom, from this voyaging,
   To counsel you, if nothing more.

" 'Twas grief oppressed you as you lay;
   Some tender sorrow which you strove
To mitigate beneath the ray
   Of this still night, some hapless love."

" Good Sir, I thank you fervently,"
   I said, "and ever must esteem
This kindness you devote to me;
   Yet, truly, it was but a dream."

"Nay, nay, my friend, let such be true;
　To keep the vision from my sight
Were weak indeed; I promise you
　We each have had a dream to-night."

He urged in tones persuasively
　Solicitous, nor longer I
Could hold my speech evasively;
　Nor choice was left but to comply.

"It was a dream of Italy,
　And in the spirit I was led
To scenes that erst were known to me,
　And cities I had visited.

"At first but dimly seen, these grew
　More bright as still I journeyed on,
Till one was with me whom I knew,
　And yet I could not see that one.

"It was a presence felt as near,
　Though all to me invisible,
As on the still and pallid air
　We swept o'er valley, stream and hill.

"At length a rosy twilight spread
　Around us in our silent flight,
And soon the sky was glowing red,
　And hills were tipped with crimson light.

"As these we passed, the opening view
    Disclosed a sunset, and its beam
Tinged a wide valley with its hue,
    And the far winding of a stream.

"Familiar in my dream it lay,
    A vale remembered but too well,
And cherished for the memory
    Of one I loved as none may tell.

"I saw the paths we used to stray,
    By meadow, slope and wooded hill,
As down the vale we held our way.
    Myself and the invisible.

"And now a seat that we had shared
    Beneath the vines, and now a tree
Where we had carved our names and dared
    To vow to love eternally,

"Appeared, and I would fain have found
    A voice my burning thought to speak,
But could not break the spell that bound
    My lips, and I grew faint and weak.

"But now a voice was in my ear
    That stirred me in the realm of sleep;
Her voice that I had loved to hear
    Now drew my spirit from the deep.

"'Oh stay! the night is very fair,
　　Stay yet awhile and walk with me,'
It said, and then upon the air
　　Her form appeared most vividly.

"In perfect feature and array
　　It bent above me while it threw,
Around the space wherein I lay,
　　The radiance of its snowy hue.

"And, gazing on me silently,
　　It moved and thrilled me with surprise,
For as it went it beckoned me
　　With tenderly beseeching eyes.

"'Yes, yes,' I cried, 'I come! I come!'
　　And sprang to clasp it, but awoke,
As echo whispered in my room
　　The words that from my lips had broke.

"And raised upon my couch I stared,
　　Where late had shone the fervid gleam
Of the fair vision disappeared,
　　Scarce conscious all was but a dream.

"Now hope of further rest was vain,
　　And I arose to seek the air
And calm my fevered heart and brain,
　　Whose pulses loud were beating there.

" Descending softly then, I pressed
 The latch, and found the simple door
Obey my touch, and then I blessed
 Such guileless ways and sought the shore.

" The rest you know, or may surmise;
 The grief were guilty that could bear
The sheen of these resplendent skies
 Unmoved, nor find some solace there.

" Not such is mine; and yet the cloud
 Returned full soon, for 'twould appear
That as I came I mused aloud,
 And broke on your retirement here."

" I bless the chance that brought you so,
 My friend; our meeting well may be
A pleasure I would not forego,
 Which speaks to me of Italy.

" But more of this again, for I
 Have hopes that centre there in one
For whom in wasting age I sigh,
 And pray, and fear, and still hope on.

" Meanwhile I gladly would assuage
 The grief that fills your anxious breast;
Why should this idle dream engage
 Your thoughts and break your spirit's rest?

" Your love is crossed; all great loves are,
  If half the tales we read be true,—
But fate remits her cruel war,
  And love survives to visit you.

" All seems propitious by this sign;
  Take courage, you may yet be wed.
Thus would I read the dream if mine."
  "Ah, Sir, that loving friend is dead,"

I made reply, and looked where shone
  The moonlit river's broad expanse,
More privately to muse upon
  The story of my sad mischance.

But soon again the agèd spoke.
  " Forgive, Oh pray forgive the jest
My foolish tongue so rashly broke;
  Forgive my folly and request.

" Too well I know the grief that pains
  The heart that mourns an absent one;
Of all that dwell upon these plains,
  I deem myself the most alone.

" For I have mourned each early friend,
  Wife, children, too, most dearly loved,
And but for one would wish to blend
  My dust with theirs and be approved.

" Man's consolation may be vain
   To turn the tide that sorrow pours
For those we ne'er may see again,
   But all my sympathy is yours."

" And I shall prize it much," I said,
   " And this our interview shall be
Preserved as with the saintly dead,
   Long, long within my memory.

" Still, if I may presume to name
   A wish that urges me to try
Your goodness further, I would claim
   The knowledge of your history.

" This tranquil shore and thoughtful moon
   Invite us to prolong our stay;
I pray you then to grant the boon,
   Some hours are yet until the day."

" My son, I would but ill requite
   Your trusting confidence if I
Declined the task; and yet, to-night,
   I well may pause ere I comply.

" For often as this moon returns
   And harvest time, recurs the date
Of an event my spirit mourns,
   And I come here to meditate.

" But what of life can e'er reveal
　The current of another's years ?
We truly know but that we feel,
　Our joys and sorrows, hopes and fears.

" Then to my task, and may it bring
　You change of thought the while I trace
My gayer course, when all was Spring,
　And I a stripling in the race."

He said, and pausing, oft he threw
　A glance where bright the river ran,
As if to bring the past to view,
　And then the sage his tale began.

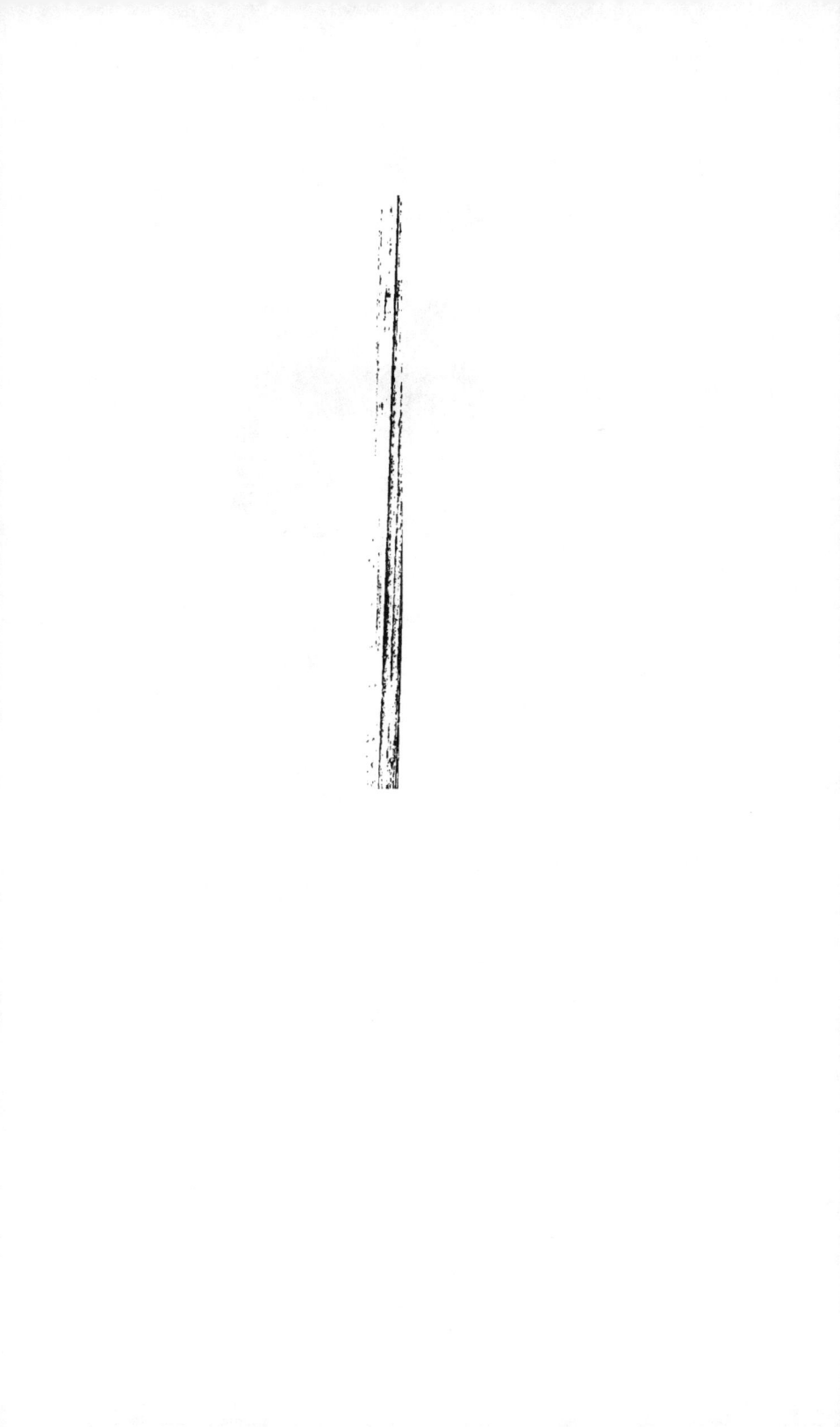

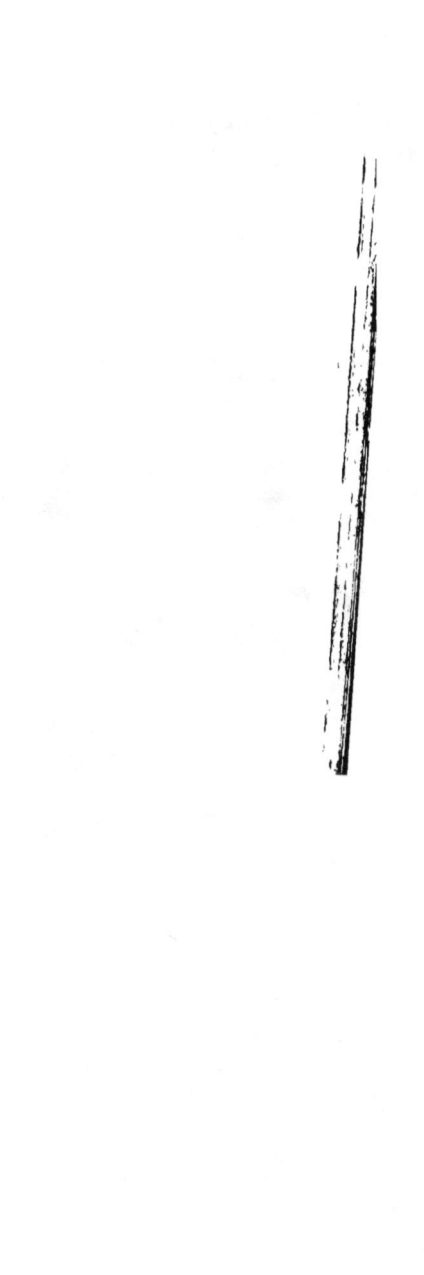

I.

My hour is near the noon of night,
My locks are grey, my beard is white,
My brow is seamed, and grief and care
Have ploughed my very spirit bare,
And quenched the fiery glow was there
  In flush of youth and manhood's prime,
Till heart, and brain, and nerve betray
The course of nature's swift decay;
And even the power of memory
  Is waning now, save for the time
Of glowing youth's impassioned day
  Of high resolve and hope sublime,
Ere reason shaped my future way,
  Or I had left my native clime
Forevermore to be exiled
From all that knew me when a child.

Renewed in all the force of truth,
The vision of departed youth
More fresh in retrospect appears
Than all the intervening years;

And I but take the sign to be
That new approaching infancy
That comes with age and failing powers
To soothe us in the languid hours,
Till we may rest where rest is sweet,
And life's full circle is complete.

But cease the plaint;—to-night I'll be
Once more a wayward boy for thee,
A thousand leagues across the sea,
    Though scores of years have come and gone,
'Mong hills where streams with laughter leap,
Resounding down the rocky steep
To birchen glades and valleys deep,
And floods of tranquil gleam that sleep
    In the heart of brave old Caledon.

But how each various charm portray
Of haunts I loved in that young day?
A simpler aim be mine, to trace
    Whate'er of note the life may give
In that green vale wherein my race
    For ages long were wont to live
In feudal guise, with much of pride,
Enclosed from all the world beside.

My home that in the midst arose,
    No bright, delicious silvan bower,

Inviting calm and sweet repose,
  But a rough, gaunt ungainly tower
That on a rocky mound was set,
  And told of strife and vanished power;
While down the slopes there lingered yet,
Of ancient stem, but leafage green,
A few old oaks to grace the scene,
And yews that furnished many a bow
In far off days of long ago.

But save this rugged tower on high,
All else was verdure to the eye,
In gentle, undulating swell;
And if upon the ear there fell
A note to break the stillness round,
'Twas but the brook that babbled by,
In circuit wide below the mound;
Or, wafted fainter, sweeter still,
The sheepbell's tinkle on the hill
That made the stillness more profound;
Or, plaintive o'er the valley wide,
The lowing kine at eventide.

Romantic vale; nor less the race
That knew it as their dwelling place,
In patronymic bond and dress,
And badge plucked in the wilderness.
No dread had they, or but that shame

Should light upon their ancient name,
In honour held by field and flood,
For deeds of Highland hardihood,
From pristine days, when by the sword
Their rights were held; and their strong word,
A tower of faith in any cause
Beyond their rural code of laws.

The sterner virtues thus possessed,
With much of chivalry were dressed,
That to their native valour lent
A most exalted sentiment
Of reverence with devotion true
Unto their chief; what more would you
In Albion's host of martial sons?
And for the other gentler ones
That beautify the cares that vex,
They could be gentle to the sex
And youth of kin, and were sincere
In friendly, hospitable cheer
To strangers; none so scant but he
Some deed of gentle courtesy
Would shew, and with a truer grace
Than oft is found in higher place.

Gone are those hardy spirits now,
Those stately forms with martial tread,

O'erwhelmed in war's tumultuous flow:
Alas, their very name is dead
Throughout the vale; the phalanx bled
On wild Culloden's fated field,
With their grey chief who scorned to yield,
Preferring death; they proud to go
Where'er he led against the foe.

And thus the clan, reduced and faint,
Fell to my sire with name attaint
And forfeit lands, until that he
Might win the royal clemency
By dint of merit, and atone
For past misdeeds and favour gone.

It chanced when swept the tide of war
  To this fair region of the West,
And, lured by fate, or fortune's star,
  We dared the prize from France to wrest,
A day of welcome tidings came
To such as were of Highland name,
And under ban of penal laws
For arming in Prince Charlie's cause;
That for good service, loyal and brave,
The crown all forfeitures would waive,
And lands and civil rights restore
With honours larger than before.

Then at his beck unto the hall,
  As if by touch of magic wand,
Came fifty warriors, lithe and tall,—
  The gallant remnant of the band,—
To leave their native shore for aye,
  To battle in a foreign land,
Or Canada, or far Cathay,
  Or where the flag should be unfurled,
They little recked, but would obey
  To follow him throughout the world.

Obedience is a monarch's bliss,
And hireling sword, and lives are his,
  The duty that awaits on thrones;
But hearts attuned to love like this
  He may not buy and rarely owns;
Or if he wield the magic power,
'Tis lost in some unguarded hour,
When love may turn to hate and bring
Destruction and dethrone the king.

Devoted these as wish could claim;
The kindred ties of blood and name,
That more than all the Gael reveres,
The legends of a thousand years,
That native bard could well employ,
What change of fortune could destroy?

'Twas ever thus from sire to son.
Strange fate 'tis mine to speak of one
I never knew by mortal sight;—
But ever to the mind he seems
As pictured in my childhood's dreams.
Their leader in the gallant fight
That captured Stadacona's height.
And this wide land to Britain's sway,
On that most memorable day,
When fell the heroes,—Wolfe, Montcalm,
On the proud Plains of Abraham.

'Twas when the plaided Highland ranks,
Like a great wave that bursts its banks,
Dashed o'er the plain with eager speed,
That one of them was seen to lead,
Of shapely mould, in manhood's Spring,
And in his cap an eaglet's wing
Denotes the ancient rank he fills,
As when he trod his native hills.
Impetuous, lithe and free of limb,
  Their claymores flashing in the sun,
A thousand swords they follow him,
  A thousand hearts that leap as one
With his; what martial feat more brave?
To meet the long steel crested wave,
That rolling onward, nearer, higher,

Now bursts a volleying line of fire!
But as they near their veteran foes,
And dart intrepid to the close,
A volley flies, and now a shot
That peals a louder, deeper note,
Ploughs through their ranks a ghastly lane,
And he that led bleeds on the plain.

Oh sad and fatal day for all
The kindred band that saw him fall,
And would have died his life to shield;
No time to pause on that red field
Ere yet the gallant fight were done,
    They swift to vengeance onward passed,
Nor stayed their hand till all was won;
    But ere they knew the die was cast,
My sire his earthly course had run,—
    Their youthful chieftain and their last.

Oh sad and fatal day for all
That dwelt near his deserted hall,
When came the tidings of the fight;
Sad day when first I saw the light,
A child of fate untimely born,
    'Mid wail of grief and wild despair
Of widowed heart by anguish torn,
    Whose joy had been his constant care,

That ne'er before had left her side;
  Alas, and she so young and fair,
And but three years had been a bride,
When on my natal day she died.

One other child the pair had blessed,
Their first delight, the heir possessed
Of all their hopes; two summers he
Had grown in happy infancy
When thus bereft; Oh, fatal morn!
Two babes, and one but newly born,
No mother's tender love to share,
Nor yet to know a father's care
In headstrong youth, the curbing hand
To guide, admonish, or command,
Ere passions grew to fill the breast,
And vex the life with their unrest,
As fretful storms to ruin bring
The fairest promises of Spring.

But never lack of love we knew,
Our mother's kin were leal and true,
And we were nurtured as became
The scions of the race whose name
We bore,—the heirs of him that stood
The highest of that name and blood.
For each some rival claim would press

In turn to fondle and caress
The orphans, and the duty share
Of rearing us, cast on their care
So young; and, good or ill betide
Between their pity, love and pride,
They saw no fault in us to chide.

It was a joyous time as e'er
To children fell, so void of care
And irksome rule, and still its power
Is with me in the twilight hour,
As musing, oft I seem to see
The faces that have gazed on me
And smiled upon my childish glee.
And, strange as it may seem, I grew
The hardier, bolder of the two,
With skill in every sport that lures,
And youthful spirit that endures.

Old Allan was our friend and guide
In use of arms, and much beside
That youth delights in, and his pride
Was that he taught alike our sire
His boyish sports, ere yet the fire
Of his own day had fled, and he
Had followed him beyond the sea,
Fought by his side and saw him fall,

Alone returning to the hall
To hang his claymore on the wall
And serve his sons; there tell the tale
Of battle to the listening vale,
   Well pleased to shelter in its breast;
An exile's lot the worst of ills,
   Scarce deeming that his bones would rest
Beyond the circle of the hills.

A faithful counsellor in sooth;
But age is slow and tame, and youth
Impetuous as a broiling stream
That none can stay, and it would seem
I chafed beneath his wise control.
And slighted too the honest soul,
Despising rule and maxim sage
As holding me in tutelage.

For I had then to manhood gone
   Some twenty summers, and was knit
With sinewy strength, displayed by none
   Of equal years; for, saving wit,
I was full grown as now; Ah me,
I stood a fair and stately tree,
   With crest aloft and flourish meet;
Pray you forgive the simile;
   'Tis long since youth, and I but greet

Its image in the blooming time,
  Ere tempest and the lightning heat
Of passion dimmed its glorious prime.

For thus it was, and in this wise
It fell; two brothers' trustful eyes
On one fair face were bent, whilst each,
Unconscious of the other, strove
To please the maid and win her love,
And I, all confident of speech,
In such impassioned words as came
Untutored from a heart of flame,
No thought of rival had, nor sign
Perceived, and I would call her mine,
Nor was denied; so that it seemed
That it was all as I had dreamed,
Till on a day at darkling hour,
When home returning from the moor,
I met with tidings in the vale
That they were to be wed,—the tale
Was on each gossip's lip,—and I,
Amazed and stung with jealousy,
Strode on in angry haste and wound
Up the steep pathway of the mound
To seek my chamber in the tower
And ponder on the evil hour;
But, dire mischance that it were so!

Ere I had crossed the slight plateau
To gain the portal of the place,
I met my rival, face to face.

Mischance?—forbid that I should screen
My grievous fault; 'twere base to lean
On subterfuge; truth, honour, love,
And all that kinship would approve,
Alike my hateful rage condemn:
I make no plea, but yield to them.

We met, and I for greeting gave:—
" So, you are not content to have
The vale, and much of all beside,
But you must rob me thus," I cried.
" Of her whose love I had possest;"
Then rose the savage in my breast,
And, springing with an agile bound,
I closed him in my arms around,
Resistless strength in my despair,
A moment poised him in the air,
As some slight thing, or senseless clod,
Then dashed him prone upon the sod.

Ah me, 'tis well some blessed control
Clings to the passionate of soul
When pride and ire to madness urge,

Or I had cast him o'er the verge,
Upon the deadly rocks below,
My first intent, and even now
I feel appalled to think I stood
So near to shed a brother's blood.

Henceforth we dwelt apart; for each,
   Long years must silent ebb away,
And seas divide us, ere the breach
   That wide and deep between us lay
Could heal; aught else seemed vain to teach
   Forgetfulness of that rude day;
He bruised at heart with cause so strong;
I harbouring a fancied wrong.

And he was of a gentler mood,
   And comelier far to look upon
In hall or vale; was brave and good,
   And courtly as a Spanish don;
So generous in brotherhood,
   That had he lost and I had won,
He would have loved me none the less,
   But manfully have borne his fate,
Or even joyed at my success,
   So far was he removed from hate,
So perfect in all nobleness
   Of heart, and gallant, yet sedate;

No marvel he was deemed to be
True knight of Highland chivalry.

Now he was changed beyond recall,
And there was silence in the hall;
No playful word, no cheering tone
Its stillness broke; his tread alone
Fell on the ear with dismal sound,
That echoed through the chambers round,
And kindred spake with bated breath,
As if it were the house of death;
Nor me addressed, save with a glance
Of mute reproach, a look askance
That told how deeply I had proved
Their hearts for him they dearly loved.

But fortune came to aid my scheme,
For still my thought was but a dream,
When home again unto the vale
Came one with many a welcome tale
Of this far land for which our kin
Had bled, and of their homes therein.
On the great River's bank, where they
Now dwelt in peaceful husbandry,
And mingled ties of blood with those
Whom erst they conquered as their foes.
And brave the land in summer prime,

As he beheld, and fair the clime;
Ethereal brightness were the skies,
And Autumn with a thousand dyes
In pageantry arrayed the woods
And decked the margins of the floods
And smiling farms: and still he told
Of breadth of lands a little gold
Would buy; the lordship and the fief,
Surpassing many a Highland chief
In antique rights; that more remote,
A region lay of wondrous note,
With deep primeval forests spread,
And lakes, like ocean floods, the head
Of this great stream, and 'mid the tract
Thundered the mighty cataract.
Beyond—a world of mystery.
Of waving, treeless plains and sky,
Stretched to the hills towards the sea,
Vast, unexplored. On every hand
'Twas thus he pictured all the land
Of which he knew or yet had heard.
A thousand leagues as flies the bird
From East to West, from tide to tide,
The land for which my sire had died.

On this my firm resolve was ta'en
That I would from my country go,

Nor ever view its shores again,
And all that I had loved below;
For better it were even so
Than to behold the wedded twain,
And they and I estranged, yet near
  In all our course of life to come.
Perchance in some succeeding year,
  When distant from my native home
And all the joys that erst were dear,
  Our hearts with pride now closed and dumb,
Relenting would rejoice to keep
O' ' ties, though severed by the deep.

And thus it is that I am here,
Recounting to a youthful ear
The course of all my bygone day—
I am the Lord of Lanoraie.

II.

And here he paused and gazed intent
Upon the flood, with forehead bent,
And all forgetful seemed to be
Absorbed in deepest reveri
'Twas not the beauty of the   ;
  Nor yet the splendour of the stream.
That held enwrapt his mind and eye,
  Whate'er the purport of his dream;
But some mirage of memory,
Recurring to his heart or brain,
Had sprung to vivid light again.

At length a sigh the stillness broke,
His gaze relaxed, the dreamer woke,
And turned with wistful glance to see
My look of deep expectancy.
Then all alert his accents ran:
"Forgive an absent-minded man.

A mansion all ablaze with light,
Its radiant gleam upon the night,

A home as fair as well could be,
The *manoir* of my seigniory,
With garden decked and ample grounds,
And many a league beyond their bounds,
Of settled lands in endless chain,
A fertile and a wide domain,
From where this shining river glides
Back to the distant Laurentides.
My lordship came by having wed,
Ere my first year of exile fled,
The heiress of the Seigniory,
Of lineage from old Normandy,
The last of the de Lanoraies;
The manor from the early days
Descending by inheritance,
With patent from the King of France.

'Tis fifty years and something more
Since first I sailed along this shore,
And drew my boat upon the beach
To visit lands I thought to reach
Upon the North, perchance to buy
The fief of Sieur la Durantaye;
But fortune, chance, or some kind fay,
That had my steps in charge that day,
To meet with her that was my fate,
Led me unto a garden gate.

My hand was on the latch to win
Due entrance, when I saw within
That which made me to hesitate.—-
A maiden bending and half hid
Amid the flowers, and then I heard
Her voice, the carol of a bird
Surpassing, seeming to forbid
Intrusion; till her song should cease
I dared not break upon her peace,
She seemed so joyful and content,
And so upon the gate I leant,
Subdued and still, to hear her song.
I knew imperfectly her tongue,
Though afterwards I learned it well
From her own lips. At length the spell
Ceased, as all silent she arose,
And 'mid the stillness and repose
I knocked; at which she turned her eyes
And answered by a quick surprise,
Expressed in every limb, as she
Swift down the path came trippingly,
As if she had expected me
That day and hour; then checked her pace
As she drew near with radiant face,
A marvel of delight and grace,
All decked in robe of glistening white.

" As she
Swift down the path came trippingly."

Blue eyed she was and very fair,
A dash of sunshine in her hair;
My own was then as dark as night.
And I was dazzled, nor could stir,
And scarce a word could say to her,
Though to explain I had essayed,
For gazing on the blushing maid,
When with a drooping glance she said:
" Then be your errand what it may,
You're welcome, Sir, to Lanoraie."

Thereat the gate was opened wide,
And we were walking side by side
Down flowery paths, a youthful pair,
Fanned by the fragrant summer air;
And if my eyes looked down to see,
Or if her glance stole up to me,
'Twas that a change had come to each
That needed not the aid of speech,
Nor marvelled we it should be so,
Who strangers were an hour ago.
The heart-beat's sympathetic glow,
The gentle mien, the trustful gaze,
And love's own tender, thoughtful ways
Came in that hour to her and me,—
A love not born on land or sea,
But ever was, shall ever be,—

3

Ours through the sunshine and the tears
Of all the many numbered years
That wait on youth; the wealth untold,
The coinage of the heart's pure gold,
Forever new, forever old.
Sweet Ernestine de Lanoraie,
When I forget that blissful day
This withered frame shall turn to clay
   And they shall lay me by your side,
For all that's mortal must decay;
   But love is strong and will abide.

But let me not anticipate
Too far; our passage from the gate
Was bright with flowers:—beyond these
The manor-house, o'ertopped with trees.
And here a dame received me well,
And I forthwith my tale could tell
Of landing on the river shore,
How chance had brought me to her door
To seek direction, or a guide,
To lands upon the northward side.

Then spoke the dame most graciously:
" My ward and I but rarely see
An unfamiliar face, or greet
A stranger in this calm retreat,

And we the more appreciate
The privilege, and duly wait
To serve you with a guide. To-day
Our fittest man we sent away
On our affairs; some brief delay
We cannot well avoid, 'twill be
To-morrow or next day ere he
Return; no better could be found
Than *Jean*, who knows the country round
For many leagues. My niece and I,
Meanwhile, due hospitality
Must offer you; 'twill please us both."
Be sure that I was nothing loath
To put their kindness to the proof
And dwell a guest beneath their roof,
And near to her whose smile betrayed
Approval of each word was said.

My joyful thanks were soon expressed.
The kindly dame then bade me rest
While they refreshment would prepare,
Albeit 'twas but country fare
They could provide; and then alone
I sat in thought, for they had gone,
And with them half the light of day
Seemed fled, till turning to survey
The room, I found there many a trace

Of her, the brightness of the place;
In portraits of her vanished race,
In music and embroidery,
And implements of archery,
For use, that in an alcove leant;
A harp, that grand old instrument,—
The poet's theme, the minstrel's pride,
That promised song at eventide.
And cabinets of books were there :—
Boileau, Corneille, Racine, Molière,
De Sévigné, Rollin, Saint-Pierre,
With many another prized to-day
For learning, poesy, and wit;
And in a volume I found writ
A sweeter word to me than lay
Or tale of theirs can give I ween.
The lovely name of Ernestine.

'Twas thus the revelation came,
And as I read it chanced the name
Escaped my lips unconsciously.
I knew not she was standing by;
But as I raised my head her eye
Caught mine, and then we laughed away
The incident, as lovers may.
And then she said 'twas most unfair
That I should know it, nor declare

My own, since now I was her guest.
" Oh, mine is Colin, and the rest
If you will have is yours as well."
Just then the tinkle of a bell
Our ears assailed, and she at last
Remembered that her errand was
To bid me come to their repast,
Which now awaited us within,
Therefore we must no longer pause;
So I forthwith was ushered in;
Madame appointing me a seat
Upon her right, as was most meet,
And opposite to Ernestine,
While she presided like a queen,
Compelling homage, less by art
Than graceful service from the heart,
Grateful to mine. It was, withal,
A bright and tasteful dining hall,
Hung with old pictures of the chase,
And where they left a vacant space,
Two swords were crossed upon the wall.
An antlered head above the door,
An antique clock upon the floor,
Telling its tale. " Now, I implore,
Lunch well, like a good *voyageur*,
And take this glass of wine, *Monsieur*,

For you have toiled upon the stream,
Where rowers may not rest and dream."

" Nay, *Madame*, with the greatest ease,
Thanks to a favourable breeze,
I sailed along from Trois Rivières.
I was so lucky as to bear
A letter from the Commandant
Which more than filled each social want
In this most hospitable land;
For I was passed from hand to hand
Among his friends, most genial, kind;
But I into your world came,
Without a missive or a name
To herald me, and was received,
Unquestioned, honoured and believed,
And 'n your hearts a place I find,
And I shall ever bear in mind
Of all my other days the day
You welcomed me to Lanoraie."

" Ah, now, *Monsieur*, you do but jest,
We are but country folk at best,
And you come from the Citadel
And all the gaiety as well
Quebec affords. Is it not thus?
Indeed I fear you flatter us

Too much. 'Tis pleasant to have friends ;
In rural life they make amends
For its seclusion; ours are wide
And far along the country side,
A league or two apart; we try
As we have opportunity
To the old friends to add a new one,
And trusting we may find a true one.
Monsieur, this glass of alicant."
"' Tis *Monsieur* Colin, my dear Aunt,
In that I am his confidant."
"Yes, *Madame,* call me, if you please,
Just Colin; ere I crossed the seas,
In my old land among the hills,
My aunts did so, and heaven wills
That you should bring them to my mind,
For you and they alike are kind."
"And had you not a mother then ?"
" Nay, *Madame,* never to my ken,
Nor yet a sire, for he was killed
With Wolfe upon the Plains; they filled
The place of both. I've heard it said
That when my mother knew him dead
She perished too, by grief outworn,
The day and hour that I was born."
" Poor child ! how very sad ; we too

Have suffered much the same as you.
Her grandsire bled upon the plain;
My brother also there was slain."
" Ah, *Madame*, war's a cruel school
While it doth last. This change of rule,
With every right secured, at least
I trust is proving for the best,
And will ensure our country's peace.
Between its races war must cease
Forever; for the land is great,
Beyond our knowledge now; 'tis fit
One nation should inherit it,
And build it strong on every side,
And found it deep and very wide,
And guard it well at every gate
From foes without that watch and wait;
From foes within, if such there be,
That none may mar its destiny,
And let our children's children see
We kept the whole inviolate
For them; not ours but theirs the fate
To know its stature and its strength,
To manhood's greatness grown at length,
If they in peace and unity
Hold to the land throned on the sea,
The bulwark of our liberty,

And share in its stability.
This do, and leave to heaven the rest."
" I had a grudge, my honoured guest,
Against your nation, for the cost
On that dire field, in dear ones lost:
But that has come to all of us,
And now I know that it was thus
With you, it makes our own seem less
Than 'twas before, and I confess
Your words are strong and very wise
For one so young. Now, ere we rise,
Speak Ernestine; how spend the day?
Nor make it dull at Lanoraie
For this our guest, which I much fear."
" I thought of Romer, Aunt, my dear,
    Should you approve and we may take
The horses for a run that way.
    'Tis such a lovely little lake."
" It is a favorite haunt with her,
    And if, indeed, you care to ride,
Then let it be to Lake Romer."
    " I shall be charmed as you decide."
" Then children take your holiday."
Soon to the lawn I took my way
To wait her coming, where I found
Two chafing steeds that pawed the ground.

Mine was a chestnut, tall and slim,
Well suited to my length of limb;
Of racing strain it promised speed.
A pony hers, the native breed,
A black and glossy little steed,
All mettle from the head to heel,
With wealth of flowing mane and tail,
That ne'er had known the touch of steel.
As now equipped in neat array,
With riding skirt, and hat, and veil,
His mistress comes, a little neigh
He gives, and all impatient stands,
Till, petted by her dainty hands,
He gets an apple for his pains,
And she can mount and take the reins,
And we are off, and through the gate,
And up the road at rapid rate,
In joyful mood; so long confined
In stall, they emulate the wind.
The manor-house is far behind,
And each with other seems to vie
To keep the pace, though it is high;
Fence, field and tree go flitting by,
As if the earth were all awheel
Beneath their feet, and we could feel
Its motion as they rocked and ran.

And now the little farms began
With cottages to deck the plain,
And we at length could draw the rein
To canter, then come to a walk,
And then to laughter and to talk
About her gallant pony's speed,
And how he tried to take the lead,
All for her pleasure and his pride:
But there were many more beside
Who paid her homage on that day:
The *habitant* upon the way.
And in the field, as past we flew,
Politely doffed his *tuque* of blue.
The women courtesied at the door.
And trooping children, half a score,
Beamed with delight, for well they knew
La Châtelaine* de Lanoraie ;
And she would bow and smile alway,
Her greeting with a charming grace
Reflected from her form and face.
" These are your subjects loyal and true,
And all conspire to honour you."
" Not subjects, for the word offends
My ear; but rather say my friends,
For they all love me, as you see;

* The term Châtelaine is even still employed in remote districts.

Their hearts are quite enough for me."
Then half in mischief, half in glee,
At her reply away she sped,
And I must give my steed his head
To gain the distance to her side;
My admiration turned to pride,
To see how boldly she could ride
   Upon the rough uneven way,
As for a mile or two we stride,
   Till at a farm at length we stay,
And leave our horses to be fed;
Then by a path that further led
Across a meadow, through a wood,
Down to the margin of the flood.
Here grew a spreading maple tree.
Meet resting place for her and me—
A shady haunt with rustic seat,
By her devised, where at our feet
The shimmering lake could well be seen,
Girt with its shores of living green.
And much I praised the silvan scene;
And musing with abstracted air
Upon the coming time I spoke
Of Durantaye and *Jean*, which broke
My reverie. " You can't live there;
There are no people, or but few;

No manor-house to shelter you,
No village, no society,
And you would perish of *ennui*.
Oh, can you be so cruel to me?
You make us love you in a day,
And then—and then—you go away
To come no more, and I shall die."
" Confound the fief of Durantaye,
And *Jean!* they put me to the rack.
I care not if he ne'er come back;
Then be not grieved by doubts and fears.
I'll love you all my length of years."
And then I kissed away her tears,
And drew her to my beating breast,
Where her dear head was laid at rest,
And our young hearts brimful of joy,
And peace, and love without alloy,
Were stilled; and in the world around
Was silence, save for one sweet sound,
Where Rossignol, high in the tree,
Poured his love-laden melody
And woke the echo of the grove,
The laureate of our day of love.
The trees, the shores, the sun on high,
The sailing cloudlets of the sky,

A mimic world of beauty make,*
Deep in the bosom of the lake.
On graceful and untiring wing,
Now flitting by, now hovering,
Intent on its aerial food,
The blueback swallow skims the flood.
So fair the scene around, below,
So restful, time scarce seems to flow,
Till all too soon the summer day
Began to wane; we must away,
Who have a league or two to go,
Ere that the night its shadow throw
Upon the plain of Lanoraie.

And now upon the brink we stood,
And peered into the glassy flood,
To see two smiling faces there;
One with a wealth of sunny hair
Dishevelled in the depths below,
Which her deft fingers gathered now
And neatly bound. " Ere we depart,
My Ernestine, my own sweetheart,
Will you not sing a song for me,
A ballad of old Normandy,

---

* Lake Romer is much changed, its shores being long since com-
pletely denuded of trees,

Or some sweet *chanson* of the plain ?
  Or let it be whate'er you will,
So I may hear your voice again.
Our little friend upon the tree
  Is silent now and all is still."

I give the words as they were sung,
Converted from her native tongue;
But who can give the tender flow
Of music stilled long years ago?
The voice that trembled through the grove
With all the fervency of love.

I had a heart and it was free
  As any bird that wings the sky,
Or tunes its note upon the tree;
  No blither pair, my heart and I.
We roved the sunshine and the shade,
  We sang the songs that we had heard;
For I was but a country maid.
                    Sing, sing, my bird.

I had a heart without a wound,
  Nor deemed it could be lightly moved;
Alas, it was in fetters bound.
  Ere ever that I knew I loved;

Lost in an hour to one that paid
    His homage with a graceful word;
For I was but a country maid.
                        Sing, sing, my bird.

I had a heart, but it is gone
    For refuge to another breast,
For I had need of only one,
    And that had found a place to rest.
Where mine had been, and it has stayed
    To beat with rhythmical accord,
For I am but a country maid.
                        Sing, sing, my bird.

But if in durance this should pine
    For joys too great for me to know,
And discords make, sweetheart of mine,
    My own heart's tide would cease to flow;
Since all the bloom of life would fade,
    With loving smile and tender word,
For I am but a country maid.
                        Sing, sing, my bird.

I kissed her on the lips, the brow,
My thanks; I think I see her now,
As she looked up with smiling eyes,
Clear as the lake, blue as the skies;

Then, turning up the path with her,
We bade adieu to dear Romer,
A happy vision of the past,
A memory while life shall last.

Our horses chafing at delay,
We sped along to Lanoraie
Through air all redolent of hay,
And our good steeds no longer strove
In rivalry, as they had come,
But thinking of their stalls at home,
They hold together as they move
By cot and farm, and maple grove;
One star aloft, eve's glittering crest,
And all aflame the crimsoned West.

'Twas thus my love was wooed and won,
Between noon-day and set of sun,
And little more remains to say,
Save that our wondrous holiday
To its most fitting ending came,
When in the presence of the dame
Each stood abashed with throbbing breast,
In all our youthful love confessed,
Awaiting by her high behest
That doom of dread that oft befalls

4

Two anxious loving criminals,
Or sentence fraught with joy and bliss,
Remembered from that day to this.
" You are to blame; but since 'tis so
Without my leave, I will forego
Reproaches." Here displeasure fled,
And in the Autumn we were wed;
No happier pair on earth I ween
Than Colin and his Ernestine,
And there is nothing more to tell,
For all is well that endeth well.

" Nay, my good Sir and honoured friend,
But I would hear it to the end,
For, pardon me, did you not say
The course of all your bygone day
You would relate?—be not so hard,
A tale half told is ever marred."
" My son, the better part is told
And I've repaid a hundred fold
What you confided of your dream."
" Nay, Sir, I beg of you proceed,
And tell the tale as 'twas agreed;
For that untold to me may seem
The better part; above the stream
The moon still rides; most thankful I
For all your gracious courtesy."

" Then farewell all my proud reserve,
For better meed you well deserve,
Who with a patient ear could deign
To harken to so long a strain
On my fled youth; for, to be plain,
I've lived that happy time again
With you, and grateful it has been,
Recalling all the faded scene."

Here he was silent for a space;
All motionless, till from his face
He seemed to brush away a tear,
And then once more with accents clear,
And memory refreshed and hale,
He plunged again into the tale.

III.

How gaily wing the shining hours
When youth, and health, and love are ours;
The heart as light as summer air,
Without a shock, an ache, a care;
Unheeded all life's grosser ills,
For joyful hope the bosom fills,
And radiance, blissful and sublime,
Illuminates the coming time;
While conjured scenes of splendour rise,
To lure us with their sorceries;
Ambition's airy dreams that fill
The mind, and captivate the will
To their achievement; my domain
Was wide, but wider in the brain
The broad estate I planned and sought
To make one whole with Lanoraie.
Upon the Eastward side Dautray,
Of many leagues, and it I bought

Within a year or two, and brought
A higher culture to the soil
Than was its wont; the peasantry
In emulation strove to vie
With my own manor-farm; their toil
Was well repaid, and thus was spread
Improvement, as the way I led,
Slowly at first, but in the end
Extending o'er the plain to lend
A richer hue and fresher green
To harvest fields than erst had been;
And I was vain, and Ernestine
Commended and rejoiced with me.
Now children prattled at her knee
And claimed her heart, for we had born
One son, two daughters; like the corn
They grew apace and throve, and each
Our semblance bore in looks and speech;
Dark eyed the son, as lilies fair
The daughters, with her eyes and hair.
In childhood tended, taught by her;
In close companionship they were
A source of many joys, for they
Repaid her love and would obey
Her slightest wish; their early bent
Was musical; their instrument

The harp, and her accomplishment
Became their own, and their reward
For graver tasks; each later shared
A tutor's more efficient care,
And what of time that I could spare
To mould them for the destiny
I had in view, for I would be
The founder of a family
Of high estate and prospects grand,
And future magnates in the land.

My purpose throve, and I was sent
By *censitaires* to parliament,
And read the laws, and in debate
Held no mean place; early and late
I sought distinction, aiming high,
Was ever in the public eye
A man of mark, till called to fill
A seat in Council at the will
Of higher powers; thus fortune smiled,
And I was Honourable styled,
A coveted reward; then turned
Again unto the land and burned
To make the heritage complete,
As I had planned; though scarce discreet,
I bought the fief of d'Orvilliers,

Which runs with lines of Lanoraie,
Some three square leagues of earth and sky,
Less for its use than symmetry.
Alas, what follies we commit
In our ambitious schemes; our wit,
Oft strained, at length goes to excess,
And then we miss our aim,—success.
Of land I could have done with less.
But now, most cherished dream in all
My planning, I would build a hall,
A manor-house commensurate
With my enlarged and proud estate
And dignity; the old seemed poor
And ill devised, and all the nore
That I would lodge and entertain
Distinguished guests, *à la rigueur*,
In short would play the *grand Seigneur*.

To rearward, rising from the plain,
Is Castlehill, a borrowed name
From my old Highland home, the same
I gave it when a first I came
To Lanoraie, and I would rear
This mansion on its summit where
It would be seen for miles around,
And plant and ornament the ground

With hedges, park, and all things meet,
Like a grand old-world family seat.
Foundations laid, the masonry
Arose beneath my watchful eye;
And then a sudden pause that left
The whole unfinished and bereft
Of further aid, a monument
Of my ambitious, proud intent, —
　　Not then perceived, but in the light
Of after time, and an event
　　Which came to dazzle and excite
My vanity, and turn the mind
To gain distinction of a kind
Unknown in our colonial day
To any Seigneur of the land;
By invitation or command
To entertain at Lanoraie
His grace of Clarence, who then lay
With his brave ship at old Sorel,
Great Britain's sailor Prince, so well
Remembered, who was later known
As the Fourth William on her throne.
I would a fairy scene create,
A splendid ball, a princely fête
With every joy and gay delight
I could devise, and would invite
The Seigneurs o'er the country wide.

And all the notables beside
In state affairs; what though the cost
Were large, to be a Prince's host
Once in a life were greater far
Than hoarded wealth; my rising star
Shone brightly; such pride's votaries are.

And now apprised of the event,
The Prince a gracious message sent,
That he most gladly would attend,
And if it pleased me he would send
His own band of musicians, lend
His flags, or aught else in his power
That would enhance the festal hour.
And then the Seigneurs, far and near,
Their stately dames and daughters fair.
The Governor at the Citadel,
The Aides and Commandant as well.
And every gallant officer,
Judge, bishop, priest and presbyter,
Invited were to meet the Prince.
That never met before, nor since.

And there was bustle all about
The manor-house, within, without;
Though it was small for such a rout,
The grounds were large and could be decked

In August with a good effect.
Bright coloured lamps hung in the trees,
And on the grassy lawn marquees;
These for refreshments; rustic seats
And tables in the green retreats.
And by some chance or lucky thought
A cannon was from Berthier brought
And planted near the landing port
By an old gunner from the fort,
Who would our loyalty evince
By salvos for the sailor Prince.
And in the grounds, but less remote,
A staff was raised from which would float
The royal standard on the breeze
Above the pines and maple trees.
Within were changes such as these:—
Removed were all the swinging doors,
And waxed for dancing were the floors
And chandeliers were improvised,
To hang above them, well devised
To hold a hundred tapers bright
And make the rooms one blaze of light.
Each mirror decked and shining pier
With roses from the garden near;
Festooned in wreaths around the walls,
And rarely known at country balls,
The loveliest flowers that e'er were seen;

This was the work of Ernestine
And her young daughters, all delight
In preparation for that night.

At length it came; Seigneurs and dames,
And daughters with the sweetest names,
With ponies all alert and fresh,
In dennet, gig, and high calèche.
From far manorial abodes,
Came rattling o'er the country roads;
And by the stream came many more,
From East and West along the shore,
And drew their boats upon the strand:
A *batteau* with the naval band
Came also from across the stream,
For those were not the days of steam,
But sail and oar, and paddle gave
The impetus upon the wave.
And now unto the ear awoke
The beat of oars with measured stroke,
In cadence as they rose and fell,
As o'er the waters from Sorel.
A launch that in the stern sheets bore
The regal emblem neared the shore,
Where I stood waiting, proud to greet
His Royal Highness and his suite,
A galaxy in peace or war,

And gallant, as all sailors are.
And as they step upon the land,
The cannon booms, and from the band
The swelling anthem peals on high
Its kingly strain, and to the sky
The standard floats; the company,
As through the grounds the way I led,
Pause in their talk and reverence pay
To royalty at Lanoraie.
Oh, proud ! Oh most auspicious day !
That on our house its lustre shed.
"A lovely scene, indeed," he said.
In truth it was a pretty sight,
A moon as fair as this to-night;
The manor-house ablaze with light,
The crystal lamps, like golden bees,
Or jewels, sparkling in the trees,
And on the lawn the white marquees.
And then the gay and gallant throng,
All interspersed and grouped among
The leafy grounds, in light and shade,
An animated picture made
That charmed the eye. At length the hall
We gain, and he with courtly mien,
As I present my Ernestine,
The pleasure claims that he the ball
May open with her in quadrille,

A dance that late had come in vogue,
I give the names in catalogue
Thus honoured:—My own Ernestine,
As beautiful as any queen
Of right; Sieur Le Moyne d'Iberville,
With Madame Hertel de Rouville,
And Seigneur Cuthbert of Berthier,
Dame Geneviève de Ramezay;
Seigneur Chartier de Lotbinière,
Madame Tarieu de Lanaudière.
Presented and in place they were;
By signal played the band outside
Upon the lawn: the windows wide
Were open, and the dancers glide
To music rythmical and clear,
And modulated to the ear,
Delighting in the grounds beside:
For, though it was the harvest moon,
The air was balmly as in june,
And all the throng with hearts attune
To gaiety and pleasure, since
The gracious bearing of the Prince
Was marked and flattering to each
With whom he danced or gave his speech,
And all were pleased. His heart now set
On witnessing a minuet
Danced by some stately dame and beau,

Who knew the mode of years ago,
In all its purity and grace;
For here were many who could trace
Their lineage from the titled race
Of nobles, vanished like a dream,
The founders of the old régime.
A pair most willingly would try
The Prince's taste to gratify,
And represent the stately dance,
As it came from the Court of France.
Seigneur Boucher de Boucherville,
Long past three score, but gallant still,
With broidered vest, white silken hose,
And silver buckles in his shoes,
A coat, gold trimmed, of azure hue,
White satin lined, a ribboned queue,
And ruffles, lace, and powdered hair,
Old gentlemen were wont to wear,
The lady, Madame Danversière,
The fairest once of all the fair,
In robe of richly flowered brocade,
Such as last century was made
At Lyons, or perchance Marseilles,
And worn till lately at Versailles;
Looped skirt, *la mode Parisienne*,
And lace of fine old valenciennes.
Hair powder, jewels, ear pendants rare,

A dame of most distinguished air.
Indeed they were a well matched pair
To dance a measure in the sight
Of royalty on that proud night,
And when a bar or two were played
By the musicians, and displayed
Assurance of the air desired
And the just time the dance required,
They stepped with such poetic grace
   And stately motion to the strain,
Of age was scarcely left a trace,
   You might have thought them young again,
So wholly were the pair inspired:
High step, *coupee*, and all the rest
Were given with so pure a zest,
The Prince was charmed; his comely face
Was lighted up till he arose
To compliment them at the close.

Renewed the ball was at its height,
And gallants gay, and ladies bright,
Float in the dance with footsteps light,
In waltz, quadrille, and gallopade,
With faces radiant and glad;
Young demoiselles in varied hue,
And officers in navy blue
And scarlet uniforms are clad.

" Seigneur, while these enjoy the dance,
Let us unto the lawn, the chance
Seems opportune to view the night
Outside, and if 'tis but as bright
As 'tis within 'twill be a sight
Remembered long; these youthful guests
   In gay attire; this fairy scene
Of beauty, where the moonlight rests,
   And mingled hues of changeful sheen,
Enchanting with its witchery;
Or is it but a phantasy
You've conjured to the eye and brain,
To vanish into air again ? "

" Indeed, Sir, you will make me vain.
Above all else I shall regard
It highest honour and reward
If I have your approval won
In aught I have arranged or done.
All praise and honour *you*; may I
Now offer hospitality,
Such as for you has been prepared,
And your example will be shared
By all my guests; without it they
Would fast until the dawn of day,
Nor murmur at the long delay."
" Then let us make due haste, Seigneur,

I promise you I can assure
An appetite." "This special seat,
Outside the throng, in calm retreat,
Awaits your Grace, and it is meet
My daughters should attend on you;
They come this way; permit me to
Present my eldest, Geraldine,
And Flora this; my Ernestine
Shall also come, and they shall see
You royally served." "Nay, pardon me,
These ladies shall be seated here.
And you shall send of the good cheer
For all; without 'twere ill deserved;
'Tis they that shall be royally served."

Now these commands obeyed, a gong
Was sounded, and the elder throng
Troup in the grounds to the marquees,
Now lighted up; while 'neath the trees
Are seated all the gay and young,
Fresh from the dance; to wait on these
Are half a score of village maids,
Decked for the nonce; each gallant aids
Them in the task; the soft moonrays
Pervade the scene; a silvery haze
Floats in the air; the music plays
A dreamlike strain I've ne'er heard since

5

And I am standing by the Prince,
Pouring him wine. Untoward fate!
How lessen or extenuate
My glaring fault, and yet be true
In what I now recount to you?

That which befell was in this wise:—
It chanced that as I turned my eyes
From my guest's face, that, gliding slow,
As ghostly forms are said to go,
A woman came in weeds of woe,
Sombre and dark, and disarrayed,
As one who from the road had strayed
Into the grounds and festive light,
Drawn by its glare; her wretched plight,
That should have won my pity, woke
My anger; when at length she spoke
'Twas in a plaintive minor key,
Begging an alms; Ah me! Ah me!
And I repulsed her. "Get you gone!
This is no place for such an one
As you."—"Hear me!"—"Begone, I say!
And seek me out some other day."

Our words in tones contending high
Aroused the guests, and then each eye
Caught sight of her, and all drew near.

With question on their lips, in fear
That something startling had occurred
To cause alarm, for they had heard
Only in part what had been said,
Their anxious faces filled with dread.

Then erect and tall amidst us all
    She stood with defiant look.
And wrathful scorn in her features worn,
    And in tones unearthly spoke:
" I craved," she said, " for a little bread
    Where the sun of plenty shone:
From your festive hall I now recall
    A prayer I blush to own:
But ere we part, and this famished heart
    Seeks solace for its woe,
What time shall tell with a fatal knell
    I'll bare before you now.
I see you here, and the flowing year
    To you its treasures bring:
Your wine glows bright in the glisteni g light
    Of a Prince's banqueting:
But take forever from this day
    My *curse* on you and Lanoraie!

" I see you yet; but your sun is set,
    And each joy is on the wane,

To which you clung, and your heart is wrung
  And shall never rejoice again;
For her whom *you* love all else above
  Shall languish, pine and die;
Ambition fled, and pride all dead,
  With her in the tomb shall lie.
I scan the page of your dim old age,
  And I see you left forlorn;
For each blooming bough is faded now,
  And I hear you childless mourn:
Foredoomed to the bier, your daughters dear,
  As lilies white are they,
In flower of youth, in the bloom of truth,
  Plucked out of the shining day.
And far from his home your son shall roam,
  To sleep 'neath Eastern skies,
And none of the land, but a stranger's hand,
  Shall close your sightless eyes.
And now, and ever from this day.
My *curse* on thee and Lanoraie!"

Spell-bound beneath her flashing eye
And words of fear, the company
In breathless awe all silent stood,
Chilled by her speech, and my own blood
Weighed down my heart like molten lead
As curse on curse fell on my head

" My curse on thee an

And doomed the loved ones of my race.
I felt her outstretched finger chase
The colour from my pallid face.
I could not move, nor make reply,
Her vengeance came so suddenly,
O'erwhelming me with dread and shame,
And self reproach: at length my name
I heard pronounced; the Prince it was
That spoke. " Seigneur, whate'er the cause
Of her wild speech, wake up and see
Her kindly cared for; it must be
She is demented." Then I found
My wonted powers, and glanced around
For some to aid. But where is she
That I would succour now? among
The guests the question sped along;
And many started to explore:
But she was never heard of more.
One moment and the moonlight shone
On her weird form, and she was gone
The next, ere there was time to stir,
As if the earth had swallowed her;
And all remains a mystery
Inscrutable: who she might be,
And whence she came, and where adrift
Was never known. Now followed swift
Upon her flight, unto our eyes,
A further portent from the skies.

All murky grew the welkin height,
The moon was shorn of half her light:
Without the motion of a breath,
The weighted air was still as death;
Where late had flowed a gentle breeze
No leaflet stirred upon the trees.
And black as night from out the West,
Careering o'er the moon's dim crest,
Came frowning clouds of evil form
And mutterings of a coming storm.
Save fitful flashes to the eye,
All light now fled the troubled sky.
In haste the fleeing company
Had sought the refuge of the hall
Ere fell the stroke; it would appal
You to have felt the sudden shock
That made the manor-house to rock,
And heard the fierce and shrieking wind
Tear through the grounds, and bow the trees,
And sweep away the wrecked marquees
Like chaff before a besom cast,
While hissed the rain upon the blast
In scorn; but that which came behind
Was more appalling to a mind
O'erwrought, when lightnings cleaved on high
With blinding vividness the sky,
And thundered heaven's artillery,

Ear-splitting peals more dread that day
Than e'er were known at Lanoraie.

Though sharp, the storm was also brief—
  A wrathful voice, a fluttering flame,
That wrought in many hearts belief
  That from the Deity it came
To seal the vision to our ken.
Its rage all spent the sky again
Was clear, and o'er the tearful scene,
More beautiful than it had been.
The moon now rode serenely bright,
The pensive ruler of the night.

Now cheeks that paled and eyes that peered
Into the storm no longer feared,
Pent in the precincts of the hall,
And neighing horses in the stall
And open sheds were forthwith brought.
For all impatiently now sought
To reach their distant homes and tell
The terrors which that night befell,
And all the gaieties as well.
But scant the words of parting were,
Though not from rudeness: but the air
Seemed fraught with mystery, and they
Looked grave that late had been so gay,

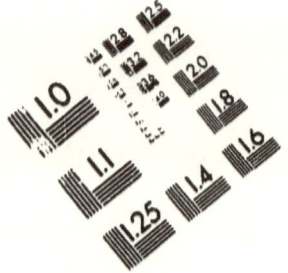

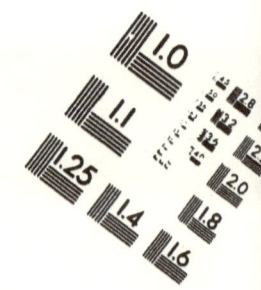

**IMAGE EVALUATION
TEST TARGET (MT-3)**

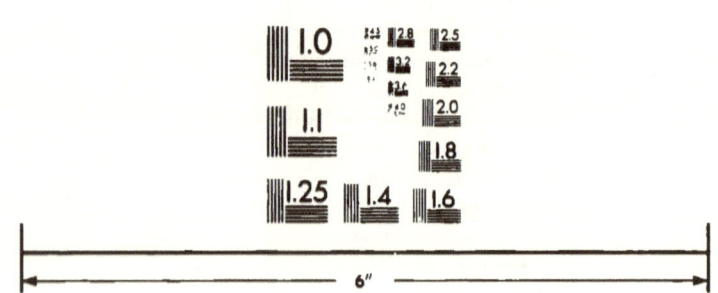

Photographic
Sciences
Corporation

23 WEST MAIN STREET
WEBSTER, N.Y. 14580
(716) 872-4503

So unconcerned and debonair,
At length the Prince and suite were there
Alone, and as the way I led
Unto the beach, the sailor said:
"Seigneur, be not cast down, the jade
Outraged all reason and is made
Of spleen, for malice is her trade;
All must have seen that she is crazed,
Or she's a witch and may have raised
The storm herself; for me and mine,
We've seen so many on the brine
It little counts; and now farewell,
And may good fortune ever dwell
With *you*, despite the witch's spell."

And thus we parted on the shore
Where we had met; well plied, the oar
Drew him afar upon the stream.
When round yon isle the launch had flown,
He waved his hand and he was gone,
One day to sit upon a throne:—
And I was with my thoughts alone.

The pageant vanished like a dream,
A tinselled show with fateful gleam
Of evil years to come, that since
I've seen befall; but then the Prince

With light persuasive words assured
The prophecy was too absurd,
And I was well content to be,
Like him, all incredulity.

IV.

There is a mystic harmony
Pervading mind, and heart, and eye,
And the pure radiance of the sky,
And the green earth, when it is joy
To live and breathe, we know not why,
Save that our hearts are in accord
With nature and with nature's Lord.
But if an evil thing be done,
This rhythmic harmony is flown,
The sympathetic chord is gone,
Or yields but a discordant tone.
If fate has shot a venomed dart,
To rankle in the aching heart,
And we are dazed and bowed with care.
We marvel that the sky is fair,
The day is bright, the fields are green,
The waters glance with sparkling sheen,
That flowers bloom, that birds can sing
And joyful soar on fluttering wing,

And all is jubilant and glad
In nature's realm when we are sad.

I grieved not for the prophecy,
Nor deemed that it would ever be
Fulfilled, the dire occasion past
That called it forth, for at the last
Calm reason came unto my aid,
And in my home no word was said
That fostered superstitious dread,
Or brought the thrilling scene to light,
So terrible that gala night;
But there would rise unto my sight,
When all was still at eventide,
The woeful one that I denied
An alms and sacrificed to pride;
The festal glare, the gazing throng,
The wonderment that found a tongue:
In every manor-house the talk
Was rife; but what could now avail?
For deeds we never can recall;
By them we stand, by them we fall.

As yet, save this discomfort, nought
    To mar my life at Lanoraie
Befell; bright skies and harvest brought
    Rich stores of wheat, and corn, and hay,

To cheer the thrifty peasantry
Against the season's change, and I
Like fortune shared; the grateful soil
Of my own manor-farms for toil
And skill returned from every field
A richer and more ample yield.
My cattle brought a fair increase
In their due season, and the fleece
Of sheep was large, and prices high
For all the fruits of husbandry.
My tithes were paid more prompt and clear
Than I had known for many a year.
All this came opportunely, since
My entertainment to the Prince
Had been at cost; but I forgot,
In the abundance of my lot,
To praise the Giver, and began
Anew to meditate and plan
My future course, as best would seem
To favour the ambitious dream
I cherished for my youthful heirs,
Entailing all my lands in shares;
Each one a manor which would be
For time in perpetuity.
To my son Hector, Lanoraie,
And unto Geraldine, Dautray,
And unto Flora, d'Orvilliers.

A home for each upon their lands,
Contiguous, ere from my hands
The whole should pass; all this had been
With the assent of Ernestine.

The Autumn fled, Winter and Spring
Had run their course again to bring
Fresh verdure to the plain, and I
Regarding my prosperity
As well assured, I gave no thought
To prophecies that came to naught.
Ah me ! but little did I think
I then stood on the very brink
Of fell disaster, an abyss
Sombre and dark, a precipice
Of fate; for I was blind I ween
To aught of evil, else had seen
The sunbright cheek of Ernestine
To pallor turn, and her sweet eyes,
Clear as the azure of the skies,
Part with their lustre and grow dim,
Like yonder moon, as o'er her rim
A sailing cloudlet steals to chase
The brightness from her shining face.
Soon it will pass, and as of yore
The splendour of her beams restore;
But Ernestine, ah, nevermore

Unto my longing gaze shall rise
The lovelight of her angel eyes
Save in the realm of paradise.

No anguish hers, no sore distress;
Nor pain, nor dread, nor bitterness
Preyed on her life; we could divine
No latent cause for her decline;
But she grew listless and supine,
And moved as one in sleep would seem,
And spoke as one would in a dream,
Or under some more potent spell;
And of the stars where angels dwell
Would talk, and from the casement gaze
Into the spangled sky, her ways
Of loving tender service past,
And I the first was and the last
To wait on her, and soothe her, till
My heart would ache, my eyes would fill
With blinding tears, as hour by hour
She drooped and faded like a flower.
And ever as her strength grew less,
All patience and all gentleness,
Content if I were in her sight,
Her hand in mine, and e'en at night,
As by her couch I vigil kept,
Held me in touch the while she slept.

And wondrous beautiful to me,
Her childlike, pure humility
To those around, when they drew near,
In their solicitude and fear,
To offer service; then her eyes
Grew radiant as the summer skies
To thank them, for she could not speak,
And on her lips and faded cheek
A smile of such felicity
Ineffable, that it might be
She saw what others could not see,
That angel spirits of the blest
Were beckoning her unto her rest.

Thus she had lived and thus she died,
And in her death was glorified
Even by the insensate clay,
As calm and beautiful she lay,
Robed in her spotless white array;
And as we gazed the glow on high,
Descending from the evening sky,
Stole o'er her features lovingly,
And touched the tresses of her hair
With radiant hues that lingered there,
Like aureola o'er her head,
Till with the setting sun it fled.

The last sad rites at length were paid,
My darling in the earth was laid;
Ashes to ashes, dust to dust,
In sure and certain hope and trust
Her spirit dwelt among the just.

Though with each throb my heart had bled,
And I was dazed with grief and care,
I could not weep in my despair,
I had no further tears to shed;
Their fountain at its source was dry,
And in my sore extremity
Brought no relief; the prophecy
Foretelling by some occult sense
This gentle yielding of the breath,
This pitiful, untimely death;—
Or was it but coincidence?
I thought of tales in Celtic lore,
Of second sight I scorned before,
Believed in by my ancestry,
From a remote antiquity;
And even yet it still was claimed
Some remnant of the gift remained
In the recesses of the hills,
Where visions of impending ills
To house, or lands, or ill-starred chief,
Oft found fulfilment and belief.

If this were so by nature's laws
I was the miserable cause
That brought the blighting curse that day,
Which slew the Pride of Lanoraie.

Years fled; my son and heir had grown
To manhood's heritage, and shown
Much of the vigor and the fire
Of my own youth; his heart's desire
Was for adventure and the strife
That animates a soldier's life
In battle fields; the clasp, the star,
Upon the breast, were grander far
Than peaceful joys and calm repose,
Or aught that civic life bestows
Of honours won in high debate
And government in halls of state;
And I had planned for his career
At home, for he was very dear
To me, and I would shield from harm
His precious life, and felt alarm
When in the forest he had slain
A bear, and at close quarters ta'en
A hurt; for all my care had been,
Since I had lost my Ernestine,
To guard our children rathe and late
Against the shafts of cruel fate.

6

Lest they should die; but since his choice
Was made I raised no further voice
Against his going, but in tears,
Remembered all these many years,
I saw him sail to cross the main,
And ne'er beheld his face again.

Now came a time when there was joy
That fed my hope of brighter days,
For if we would the mind employ
With happy thoughts and lightsome ways,
And lay the ghosts the past betrays,
On which regretful memory dwells.
That time should be when wedding bells
Ring jubilant upon the air,
And from the church the bridal pair
Are greeted by a smiling throng,
The grave and gay, the old, the young;
When children strew the way with flowers,
While radiance crowns the shining hours.
And love infolds the blissful scene.
Such was the day my Geraldine
    And Arthur de Varennes were wed;
No comelier pair was ever seen.
    And I had found a son instead
Of him that sailed across the sea,
And this was comforting to me.

But ah! the happiness was brief,
The poignancy and bitter grief
Most dire; for Geraldine was shorn
Of life when her sweet babe was born,
    And hopes were shattered in a day,
And loving hearts asunder torn
    Told of the doom of Lanoraie.

An infant daughter thus bereft,
Unto our loving care was left,
And never child so dear as she,
For in my heart's intensity
Of pity for the helpless one
I saw a fate so like my own,
Without the joy in life's sweet Spring
A mother's love alone can bring.
And Arthur heard my earnest plea
That he would grant the child to me,
My solace and my hope to be,
For I had none on earth beside
Erelong, when my dear Flora died.

"Ah, wherefore did you bid me tell
This mournful tale of what befell
My later years, when I had told
Of youth and love wherein the gold
Of my life lay ? Said I not so ?

That was the better part to know,
And not this dreary tale of woe
That nought of pleasure can impart
To you my son." " Nay, though my heart
Must feel with yours, 1 still can see
'Twere better far for you and me
That I should know the whole." " Then I,
Perforce the track of memory
Once more resume." Yes, Flora died,
My loving daughter that denied
Her pleasure to be near my side,
Where she would seemingly be glad,
Albeit that her heart was sad
For Geraldine, the more that she
Had heard the fatal prophecy
Pronounced, believing she would be
The next to go, though not in fear,
But that the child had grown so dear
To her, and would be left behind;
And while these thoughts preyed on her mind,
Her health gave way, her strength declined,
And ere another year had come
We bore her to her last long home.

In Spring when all the world is young,
  With budding leaf and opening flower,
When every brook has found a tongue,

And every bird a leafy bower,
We are reminded of the hour
Of youth and love, and sunlit ways,
And visions of long happy days,
Forgetful of the north-wind's breath,—
And that in midst of life is Death.

Yet once again his fateful dart
He threw and pierced the gallant heart
Of my son Hector, in the van
Against Mahratta and Afghan,
Pindáris hordes; thrice in the field
Promoted; he that scorned to yield
Found in these savage wilds a grave;
The only gift their land e'er gave.
Deeply I hoped that he would come
And dwell with me in his old home,
From peril and from danger far,
My race had known enough of war
In the long past; but destiny
Forbade that such should ever be ;
He sleeps far from his home and me.

Some half a score of years had flown
Since then, Eléanore had grown
A blithesome maiden; fair was she
As any dainty nymph could be

That roved the pure and sunlit air
Of twenty summers; in her hair
A glint of gold; bright eyes of blue,
With lashes long and deeper hue
Than those of stately Geraldine;
The voice of my own Ernestine,
For mellow laughter and for song,
Such as it was when we were young.
A sunbeam to my lonely hearth
In infancy; in childhood mirth,
Naïveté in maidenhood;
All innocent, and pure, and good;
A face so radiant with smiles,
Her many winsome ways and wiles
Live in my heart, and that would flee
To be with her beyond the sea.
God grant she be restored to me !

No miser prized his treasure more
Than I my dear Eléanore,
Nor watched it with more careful eye,
Lest it should vanish, than did I
Her health, till my anxiety
At each slight change grew so intense
I ill could bear the deep suspense,
And longed her safety to insure
Against the curse, and would endure

E'en separation if 'twould save
My darling from an early grave.
And it so chanced my near of kin
In the old land would soon begin
A voyage to the sunny clime
Of Italy, and there was time
To send her with them far away
From the dread doom of Lancraie.
For they and I were reconciled
Long since, and they my dear grandchild
Would gladly care for as their own,
And I could hope when she was gone.

Full sore our parting was, but still
I have endured it with a will,
More resolute of heart and mind,
Than had she stayed with me behind;
But soon or late from o'er the sea
God grant she be restored to me !

" What ails my son ? did I not hear
A sob ? and was that not a tear
Fell on my hand ? Alas, this tale
Affects too deeply, yet I fail
To catch sufficient cause; the night
Grows somewhat chill, and it well might
Tell on your nerves, unused at least

To miss so many hours of rest."
"Ah, Sir, it grieves me sore indeed
That I should cause your heart to bleed
Afresh; take courage and be strong,
My own aches sadly and my tongue
Can scarce find utterance to tell
The fate of her I loved so well.
Alas, the lost one I deplore
Is your beloved Eléanore.
Thus my misfortune and your own
Unite in her, and they are one.
Bear with me calmly while I state
This latest deed of cruel fate."

"My little lamb, and is she gone
Forever ? tell me all, my son;
The cause of it, and when, and where?
And were her friends and kindred there?
Passed she alone through death's alarms ?"
"Nay, father, but within these arms.
Her kin were present with her too,
And often she would speak of you
And Lanoraie, and bade me come
And comfort you in her old home
When all were o'er. This portrait she,
In ever cherished memory,
Sent with her love, her latest sigh

Breathing your name, and then her eye
And touch a silent parting took,
And peace and heaven were in her look."

" It is her image. Ah, sweet one,
My love, my life is now undone;
Earth has no further ills for me;
Fate has fulfilled my destiny.
The harp is silent in the hall,
   The hands that woke its chords are gone;
The sword that hangs upon the wall
   Tells of the brave departed one.
There is no heir to Lanoraie,
To Dautray, nor to d'Orvilliers;
They pass to strangers o'er the sea,
They ne'er again shall ever be
The home of any of my race,
And years will come when none can trace
The lines where stood that goodly hall,
Save by some fragment of a wall;
Or find where once a garden smiled
With flowers, but where a few grow wild
Amid the bare and desert place;
All life and love have flown away
Before the curse of Lanoraie.

7

"The moon grows faint, the morning breaks.
Your arm, my son ! this pathway takes
Us to the manor, ere the eye
Of a too curious peasantry
Is yet abroad and can espy
Us on the road; some think at least
I hold a demon in my breast
That will not let my spirit rest;
And as they pass, to guard from loss,
The sacred sign make of the cross.
Poor simple folk, they little know
'Twas exorcised long years ago.
Though I had other faults beside,
The only demon was my pride;—
That fled when Ernestine had died.
I know in whom I put my trust;
We are but creatures of the dust;
Though man is vile, yet God is just.

"Dwell with me till my course is run,
You are in every deed my son,
And had she lived she would have been
Most surely yours, and I had seen
Your life like mine with Ernestine;
And saving that I would hear more
Of my beloved Eléanore,

Such as your tidings still can give,
Most gladly would I cease to live,
Far from this earthly scene would fly,
For all my treasures are on high."

Thus told that loving man and sage,
   His joys and sorrows to his friend
Of yesternight, from youth to age,
   His erring ways and their sad end.
Not long he lingered on life's stage,
But when within the coming year
The corn had ripened in the ear,
And reapers garnered it for wage,
Reclining in the sun at noon,
And rose at eve the harvest moon;
'Twas then another Reaper came,
Late in the night his sheaf to claim—
The richest far in golden grain
Of all the harvest of the plain.
Not in his might with terrors clad,
But lovingly, and kind, and glad,
He bore in gentle arms away
The agèd Lord of Lanoraie.

I mourned his loss with tears and sighs,
And reverently closed his eyes;

For there was none in all the land
His kindred; thus a stranger's hand,
As she foretold, supplied for these
The last sad rites and offices.

And by the side of Ernestine,
His Flora and his Geraldine,
    We laid him, where the sun would shine,
Where winds would rove and skies would weep
    The dews of heaven at day's decline,
And stars their central watches keep.

www.ingramcontent.com/pod-product-compliance
Lightning Source LLC
Chambersburg PA
CBHW020803020726
47495CB00008B/2573